I Love you

to

Infinity & Beyond

PAGE PUBLISHING, INC.
New York, NY

First originally published by Page Publishing, Inc. 2017

ISBN 978-1-64138-245-8 (Paperback)
ISBN 978-1-64138-730-9 (Hardcover)
ISBN 978-1-64138-246-5 (Digital)

Printed in the United States of America

I *Love* you to INFINITY & BEYOND

ANTHONY MARUCCO

I love you to infinity and beyond,

I loved you before you were born,

Even before you were the size of a kernel of corn.

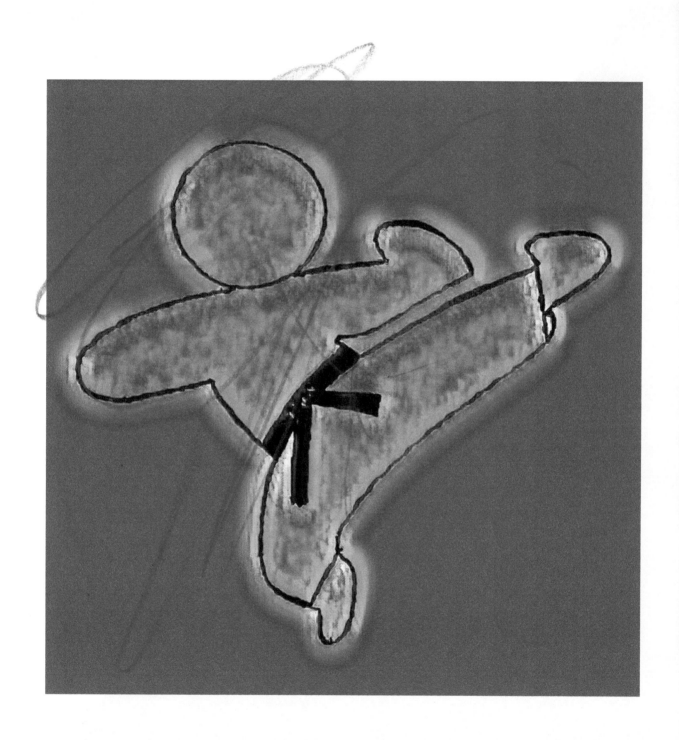

I love you when you are healthy,
I love you when you got me sick,
But loved it when I felt you kick.

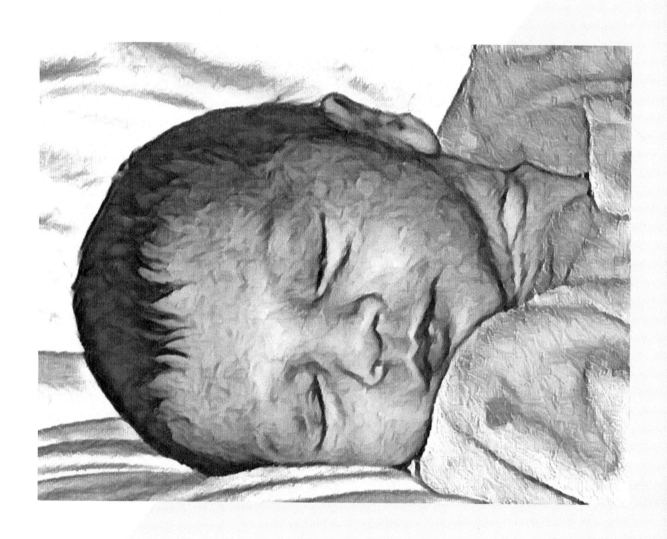

I love you when you laugh,

I love you when you scream,

But love it when you smile while you dream.

I love you when you sleep,

I love you when you are fussy all night long,

But love it when you finally fall back to

sleep when I sing our song.

I love you when you are good,

I love you when you are mad,

But love you no matter what behaviors you had.

I love you when you are happy,

I love you when you are grumpy,

But love it most when you are happy and jumpy.

I love you when you are tired,

I love you when you are a little struggle,

But love it most when you snuggle.

I love you when you are helpful,
I love you when you make a mess,
But love it when I can help you dress.

I love you when you smile,

I love you when you pout,

But love when you play peek-a-boo with a laughing shout.

I love you all day and night,

I love you all that's in between,

But love it most that I get to call you my little bean.

You are my dream come true.

There is nothing stronger than our bond,

I will always love you to infinity and beyond.

ABOUT THE AUTHOR

The author is a Licensed Clinical Social Worker with years of experience working with children and families in a variety of settings inclusive of home, schools, communities, correctional facilities, and mental health hospitals. This children's illustration book, *I Love You to Infinity and Beyond*, is the author's first published book.

This children's book began to take shape as an example during a clinical session with an individual experiencing family separation issues. The exercise "memory book" was utilized to elicit positive memories and feelings to aid the individual in overcoming their current state of feelings, as well as give an avenue to share, in some way, their memories and feelings of love and joy with their little ones.

CPSIA information can be obtained
at www.ICGtesting.com
Printed in the USA
BVHW021641040419
544556BV00001B/1/P